CW00864901

British Library Cataloguing in Publication Data.
A catalogue record for this book is available
from the British Library

ISBN 978 0 86071 895 6

A Commissioned Publication Printed by

MOORLEYS
Print, Design & Publishing
info@moorleys.co.uk · www.moorleys.co.uk

Once upon a time,
there was a tiny
lady mouse

Who lived with her family,
under a bush
outside our house.

Her home was in
the garden,
just near our back door.

Where she lived
with her children,
One, two, three and four.

They'd shout out
their names as they
stood in a row,

Eenie, Meenie, Miny and Moe.

After eating their breakfast,
and brushing their teeth,

They'd run out to play,
without stopping
to breathe.

After dinner it was lessons
and learning A B C,

Then they'd all wash their hands,
for it was almost
time for tea.

They liked to eat
sunflower
seeds for tea,

Which were put out
for all the different
birds by me.

Then after tea,
it was soon
time for bed.

But they liked to
jump up and down
instead!

Soon Daddy mouse
would appear upstairs,

So they'd all kneel
on the floor
and say their prayers.

Then dive under the covers
all comfy in bed,

And wait for
an interesting story
to be read.

After that,
Daddy mouse would
turn out the light,

Give all of them a kiss
and whisper
Goodnight.

See you tomorrow.
x x x x